For my godson Marco and niece Lia.

Always dream BIG.

To
Reagan, Lily, Stevie
& Crew,

Follow your dreams !

MERRY CHRISTMAS!!

MICHAEL DANIS

The Legend of Sappy

*A Christmas story that shows it pays to dream **BIG***

It was the day after Thanksgiving and just as it does every year, the crispness in the air created an excitement for *everyone* at Frostee's Farm.

Inside the barn, the Lennon family of cats was equally excited. Grandpa Lennon watched over the frisky kittens as they chased a pinecone around the barn. The play began to get rough as Walter pinned down Zoey, the smallest kitten in the family. Frankie and Gia watched over the scuffle, pointing and laughing.

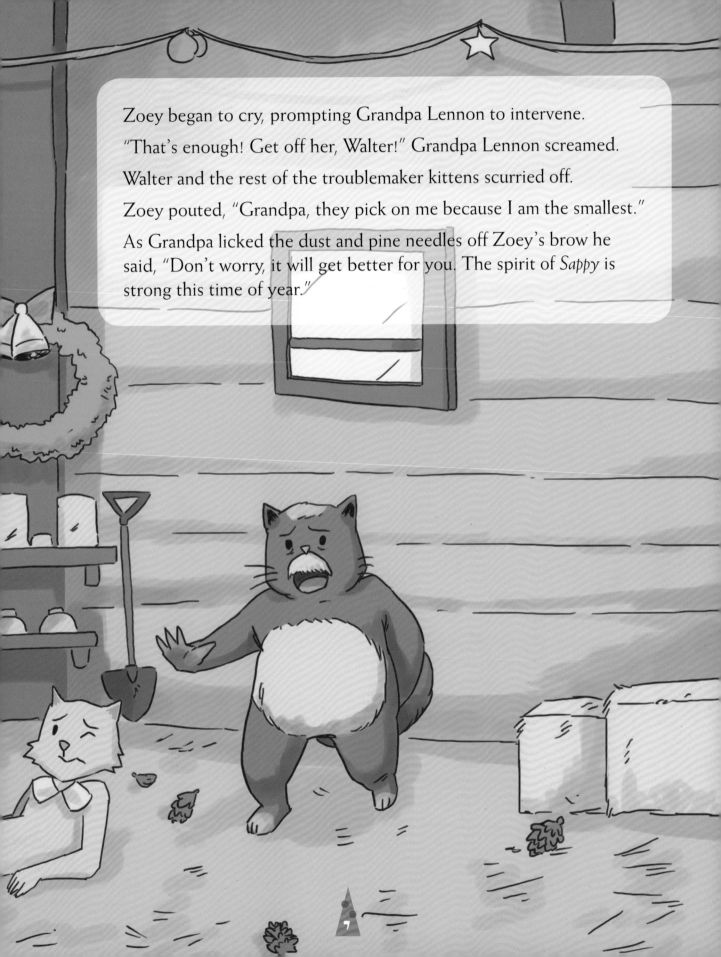

Zoey began to cry, prompting Grandpa Lennon to intervene.

"That's enough! Get off her, Walter!" Grandpa Lennon screamed.

Walter and the rest of the troublemaker kittens scurried off.

Zoey pouted, "Grandpa, they pick on me because I am the smallest."

As Grandpa licked the dust and pine needles off Zoey's brow he said, "Don't worry, it will get better for you. The spirit of *Sappy* is strong this time of year."

"W ho is *Slappy*, Grandpa?" Zoey questioned.

Grandpa smiled and said, "It's Sappy. He's a tree from the farm. Gather 'round kittens. I think it is time to share with you a story that has been passed down over the years. As you know, we cats have been an important part of this tree farm for the past century. We have kept the farm clear of pests and have allowed thousands of trees to make family Christmas celebrations very special."

The kittens stood proudly and began to listen closely to Grandpa Lennon.

"Being a Christmas tree at Frostee's Farm is risky business. Every tree wants to be chosen and dressed up beautifully."

"Beautiful like me, Grandpa." Gia curtsied playfully behind Grandpa.

Grandpa smiled at Gia and continued. "But *when* they will be chosen is the question."

S ome grow quick, Walter. Some grow slow, Zoey. Some grow tall, Gia. And some grow wide, Frankie. Beauty is always in the eye of the beholder—"

"Or the holder of the hacksaw," interrupted Walter as he jumped up to tap the saw hanging on a screw, causing it to swing.

Zoey nervously side stepped the swinging blade and gave Walter a cutting stare.

Grandpa Lennon continued. "Some trees are anxious to get off the farm and see the world."

"Like our great aunt Kittie who was adopted by that rich family?" asked Zoey.

Grandpa nodded. "Some are content to hang around the farm a bit longer and grow nice and BIG."

"Careful, Frankie!" Gia teased giving Frankie a poke in the gut.

Grandpa smirked. "The risk is that if trees hang around too long, they may grow too big for someone's house. They may never get decorated and will just become another ordinary member of the surrounding forest."

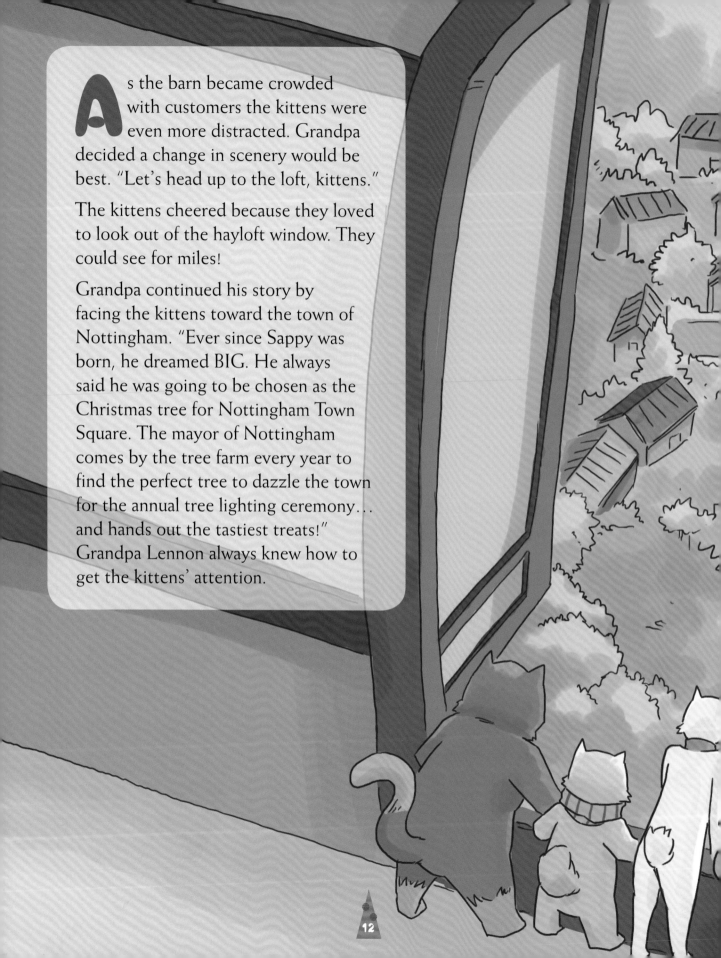

As the barn became crowded with customers the kittens were even more distracted. Grandpa decided a change in scenery would be best. "Let's head up to the loft, kittens."

The kittens cheered because they loved to look out of the hayloft window. They could see for miles!

Grandpa continued his story by facing the kittens toward the town of Nottingham. "Ever since Sappy was born, he dreamed BIG. He always said he was going to be chosen as the Christmas tree for Nottingham Town Square. The mayor of Nottingham comes by the tree farm every year to find the perfect tree to dazzle the town for the annual tree lighting ceremony... and hands out the tastiest treats!" Grandpa Lennon always knew how to get the kittens' attention.

"It's not easy for a tree to be chosen because the mayor had high standards. For starters, it had to be at least twenty-five feet tall!"

Gia proudly stretched her long legs behind Grandpa Lennon.

"And of course, the tree always had to have strong arms to hold up all the lights and ornaments."

Walter flexed his arms like a bodybuilder and gave a tough look to Zoey.

As the kittens began to snuggle in for their all too common catnap, Grandpa Lennon continued right along. He loved telling the story regardless of who was listening. "The other trees mocked Sappy and said that he would never be chosen for the Town Square because he was not well groomed like past trees."

Sappy didn't have the perfect triangle shape of a classic Christmas tree and let's not forget how he got his nickname… Sappy always drooled a bit and had sticky sap running down his trunk."

"Another tree named Lefty who had one side badly damaged in a winter storm tried to scare Sappy. 'Hey, Sappy. All it takes is heavy snow and you can end up like me.' Lefty shook his broken branches and laughed. 'Nobody wants a tree that can't hold up ornaments!'"

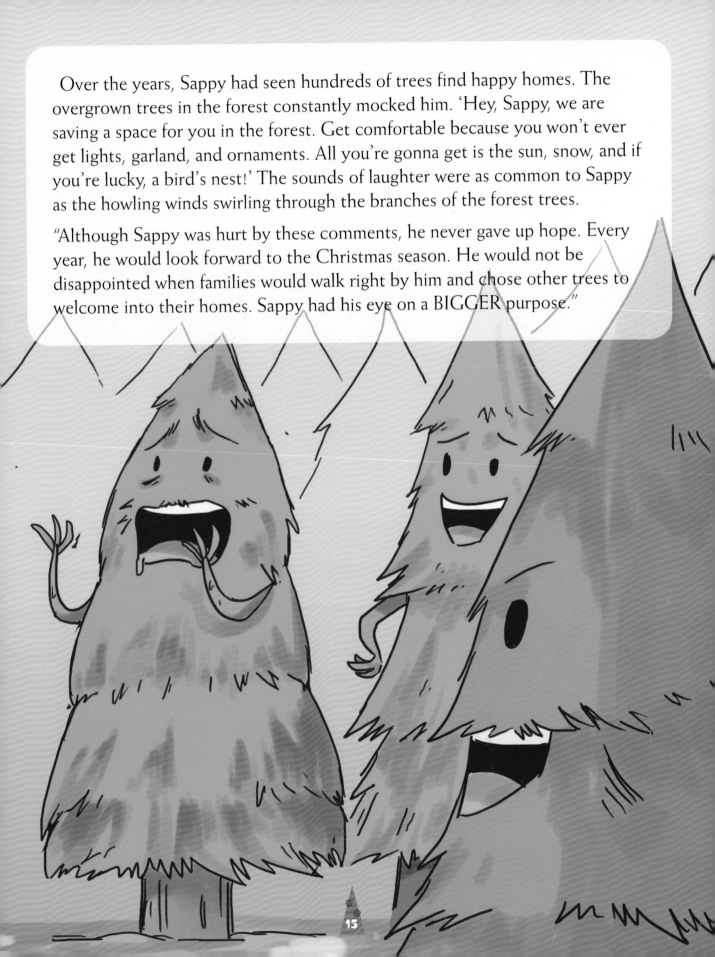

Over the years, Sappy had seen hundreds of trees find happy homes. The overgrown trees in the forest constantly mocked him. 'Hey, Sappy, we are saving a space for you in the forest. Get comfortable because you won't ever get lights, garland, and ornaments. All you're gonna get is the sun, snow, and if you're lucky, a bird's nest!' The sounds of laughter were as common to Sappy as the howling winds swirling through the branches of the forest trees.

"Although Sappy was hurt by these comments, he never gave up hope. Every year, he would look forward to the Christmas season. He would not be disappointed when families would walk right by him and chose other trees to welcome into their homes. Sappy had his eye on a BIGGER purpose."

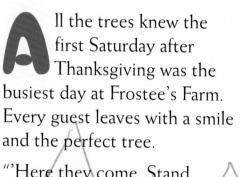

All the trees knew the first Saturday after Thanksgiving was the busiest day at Frostee's Farm. Every guest leaves with a smile and the perfect tree.

"'Here they come. Stand up straight! Give off a good smell and shake out your pine needles!' Sappy instructed the younger trees.

"'Sappy, quit drooling. What do you know about being chosen anyway? You've been here forever,' snarked Twiggy. Twiggy was a relatively new tree, only about 3 feet tall, so Sappy didn't pay him much attention.

"A couple of city slickers that spoke funny took a trip to the country for the day. 'How about this one, hon? He's kinda' cute.' She pointed at Sappy with a smirk."

"What are you nuts?" her husband replied. 'C'mon, we gotta' get a lil' one. He won't fit in our studio apartment.'

Sappy relaxed as the couple turned to Twiggy. Alright, this is more our style, babe,' she said. 'Works for me. I'll cut him down quickly,' the man agreed. 'We gotta' beat da traffic back to *Noo Yawk.*'

"Twiggy screamed at Sappy, 'See ya, sucka'! I'm headed to the BIG Apple. Have fun in the forest!'

"Sappy shrugged off Twiggy's comments quickly because off in the distance he saw what he had been waiting for. The mayor of Nottingham had arrived!"

It was quite the scene. He shook hands and kissed babies. The mayor was dressed from head to toe like he walked out of an LL Bean catalog. As he headed toward the barn to get his saw sharpened by Farmer Greg, he stopped to give out candy canes to the crowd of children and tossed a few delicious treats to the cats." The kittens heard "treats" and were suddenly listening intently again.

"After a few dozen photos, he began his march toward the tree farm to pick out the perfect tree for that year's ceremony."

"Sappy had prepared his whole life for this moment. Since he was a sapling, he had dreamed of being in the center of Nottingham Town Square. A shining tower of Christmas cheer for all the town to see. People would take his photo and sing Christmas carols beneath him. Santa would set up his throne in front and hundreds of children would come from all around town to tell him their Christmas wishes. Oh the joy he would bring!"

Sappy was finally tall enough that year to be considered by the mayor. He knew this was his BIG chance. But the next year, anything could happen. He could be damaged in a winter storm, infested by a wasp nest, or even grow TOO tall for the power lines in Town Square. The reality of the situation began to weigh on Sappy and he began to get very nervous. Unfortunately, when Sappy became anxious, he couldn't control his drooling."

"The mayor slowly walked toward the section of trees that were the right size for Town Square, pausing for photos along the way. 'You look great, Mayor,' his wife encouraged. As the mayor's team scoured the farm looking for the perfect tree, Sappy became more and more nervous.

"'This one's too fat.'

"'This one's too skinny.'

"'This one's balding.'

"'This one looks like a bush, not a tree.'

"'I think I found the winner!' yelled one of his staff. 'Come this way, Mr. Mayor!'"

To Sappy's amazement, they were pointing at *him!* Sappy could not believe it. All the years of standing in the cold, being picked on by others had finally paid off. He knew he could do it. Oh the joy!

"'Nice job, Clark!' exclaimed the mayor. 'This might be the best tree the town will ever see.' His top advisor, Clark, smiled proudly.

"Sappy bubbled with excitement as the mayor circled him.

"The photographer instructed the mayor to take a photo of him next to Sappy. Sappy was smiling branch to branch. As the Mayor leaned in and put his hand on Sappy, something terrible happened."

"'I got sap all over me! Ehh, my hands are all sticky and it got all over my brand new sweater.' His wife scrambled to get him a towel and clean up his hands. In the distance, another advisor shouted, 'Mr. Mayor, check out this year's tree for Nottingham Square!'

"The mayor looked disgustedly at Clark and said, 'Let's go see what he found. Maybe someone here *actually* knows how to find a good tree.'

"The group marched away and Sappy could not believe what had just happened. His dream was crushed."

As the years passed, Sappy's dreams of having a shining star on top of his head faded. He began to accept that he would never be a special Christmas tree. All he would ever be was just another tree in the forest.

"Sappy grew taller each year, inching closer and closer to the stars in the sky. Over time, the sting of that fateful day with the mayor subsided and Sappy began to find comfort in the smiles of the annual guests of Frostee's Farm.

"Nearly 60 years had gone by since Sappy's run in with the mayor. By then, Sappy was the tallest tree on the farm. At over 85 feet tall, he had a bird's eye view of the farm.

"One day Sappy saw something flying in the distance. He thought, *It's not a bird. It's too small for a plane. Is it Santa? Nope.*"

It was a helicopter and it was landing in the open field on the other side of the farm! Sappy then noticed a truck with a large crane that was entering the farm from the highway; it was followed by a parade of news vans. This was an even bigger scene than when the mayor visited the farm.

What is going on? Sappy wondered.

"Who was it, Grandpa?" Walter interrupted with excitement.

"Did they also have treats for the cats?" Frankie was thinking with his belly again.

"It was probably a movie star, right, Grandpa?" Gia asked confidently.

"Let him finish!!!" Zoey screamed.

Grandpa smiled at the kittens and nodded approvingly at Zoey. "Good things come to those who wait."

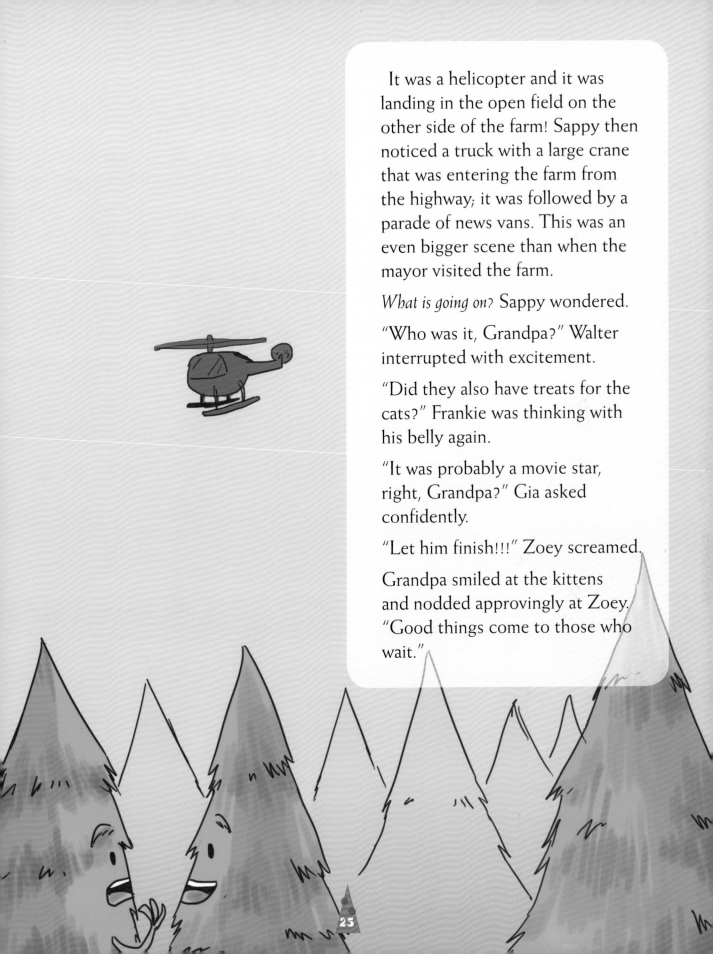

Grandpa continued, "Sappy assumed they were coming for one of the lucky trees in front of him as they did countless times over the years. People shouted 'Mr. Mayor' toward the gentleman who came out of the helicopter to greet Farmer Greg. But Sappy did not recognize any of these people. And these people spoke funny. Their accent reminded him of that couple that took home Twiggy all those years ago."

"Sappy looked down at his trunk and noticed a team putting a red ribbon around him. What happened next surprised him even more. They began to cut him down! It kind of tickled. Sappy never thought he would ever know what it felt like. He had given up on that dream years ago.

"Next, the crane hoisted Sappy onto a big truck and they covered him with a giant burlap blanket.

"*Where are they taking me?* Sappy wondered. He knew he was much too big for anyone's home or even any of the local town squares."

Sappy could not see, but felt a fierce wind blowing against his branches. They were speeding down the highway! After a few hours, Sappy was exhausted from the stress of the event and fell asleep. "

"Sappy was awoken by unfamiliar sounds. This was not the howling wind, buzzing bees, or singing birds he was used to at the tree farm. He heard jackhammers busting concrete, taxicabs honking their horns, and police sirens flying by. *Where am I?* he thought.

"When the crew removed his burlap blanket, Sappy could not believe his eyes. He was no longer the tallest one around. There were giant buildings that made him feel like a sapling again!"

As they stood him up, Sappy read the sign on the stone building that said, 'The Concourse – Rockefeller Center.' This was truly a Christmas miracle!

"Sappy looked down and saw statues of golden angels trumpeting, an ice-skating rink, flags from countries all around the world blowing in the wind, and thousands of people watching in awe."

"For the next six weeks, Sappy was dressed in 50,000 lights and topped with a star that was 10 feet wide! Famous singers and dancers performed in front of him, millions of people watched him on TV, and countless people took his picture. He would be remembered forever!"

Then, Grandpa Lennon, triumphantly exclaimed, "The legend of 'Sappy' began 75 years earlier and 200 miles from where it would eventually end. This is truly a tale of 'rags to riches' and one that shows that having patience and believing in yourself can pay off BIG in the end!"

Grandpa Lennon was so caught up in the story that he didn't realize the kittens were fast asleep for a catnap. *I guess I'll just have to tell them again next year,* he thought.

Look how far Sappy has come! He used to be known as the one who drooled on the mayor of a small town. Now he is on top of the world. It truly pays to dream BIG! Zoey dreamed.

THE END!

About the Author:

This is Michael Danis' first book. The story was inspired by a visit to a tree farm, where Michael and his wife, Michel were deciding on a Christmas tree. Their quest for the perfect tree gave way to comical critiques of the available trees. This led Michael to wonder, *imagine if these trees could hear our comments*. The rest of the story pulls from their recent relocation from New York to Maryland, Michel's experience as a third grade teacher and their family's pet cats' personalities.